just like you!

And when I grew up,
I wanted to have a little girl . . .

Just like you, I wasn't always good
and I wasn't always bad.

I was just learning to be me,
just like you are learning to be you.

I liked curtains,

just like you.

I loved to dance,

just like you.

I wanted to choose my own clothes,

just like you.

just like you.

I loved
my friends, my baby-sitters,
and my relatives,

Just like you, I liked being on top of things . . .

and getting to the bottom of things.

I didn't like certain foods,

just like you.

And, just like you,
I hated the vacuum cleaner, having my hair
combed, and kisses (except on boo-boos).

I loved animals,

just like you.

just like you.

I had a mother and father
who loved me very much,

just like you.

I slept and played,
crawled and splashed,

just like you.

I burped

and glurped

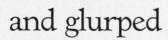

and pooped,

me   you

When I was a little baby,
I looked just like you.

To my family—
for memories lost and found
—L. T.

Printed in Hong Kong.

First paperback edition 2000

1 3 5 7 9 10 8 6 4 2
Library of Congress Cataloging-in-Publication Data
Thiesing, Lisa. Me and you : a mother-daughter album / by Lisa Thiesing.—1st ed.
p. cm.
Summary: A mother explains how much her daughter is like she was as a little girl.
ISBN 0-7868-1433-0 (paperback) [1. Identity—Fiction.
2. Mothers and daughters—Fiction.] I. Title.
PZ7.T3418Me 1997
[E]—dc21
97-27986

ME & YOU

A Mother-Daughter Album

Lisa Thiesing

HYPERION PAPERBACKS FOR CHILDREN
NEW YORK